Very Scary

written by Tony Johnston

illustrated by Douglas Florian

harcourt brace & company

San Diego New York London

Library of Congress Cataloging-in-Publication Data
Johnston, Tony, 1942–
Very scary / Tony Johnston; illustrated by Douglas Florian.—
1st ed.
p. cm.
Summary: A pumpkin shimmering in the moonlight attracts the attention
of an owl, a cat, crickets, a witch, and a group of boys and girls,
who change it into a scary jack-o'-lantern.
ISBN 0-15-298625-4
[1. Pumpkin—Fiction. 2. Halloween—Fiction. 3. Jack-o'-lanterns—Fiction.]
I. Florian, Douglas, 1950– ill. II. Title.
PZ7.J6478Ver 1995
[E]—dc20 94-10938

Printed in Singapore
First edition
A B C D E

The illustrations in this book
were done in watercolor on vellum paper.
The text type was set in Colwell.
Color separations by Bright Arts, Ltd., Singapore
Printed and bound by Tien Wah Press, Singapore
This book was printed with soya-based inks on Leykam recycled paper,
which contains more than 20 percent postconsumer waste and
has a total recycled content of at least 50 percent.
Production supervision by Warren Wallerstein
and David Hough
Designed by Lisa Peters

For Dorothy Fenner, San Marino legend,
who taught me that the English language
is really not very scary
—T. J.

For Marvin Bileck
—D. F.

One night the moon was shining, an orange, pumpkin moon. All the pumpkins by the fence shimmered in its light.

The biggest pumpkin soaked up the light till it felt full of moon.

An owl flew down like a brown leaf.
It went *woo-woo-woo* with all its
might because that pumpkin
shined so bright.

WOO

A cat came *tiptoe-tiptoe-tiptoe.*
It *purr-purr-purred* with all its might because
that pumpkin shined so bright.

Purr-Purr-Purrrrr

A little choir of crickets hopped on top of the pumpkin. They sang *creaky-creaky-creaky* with all their might because that pumpkin shined so bright.

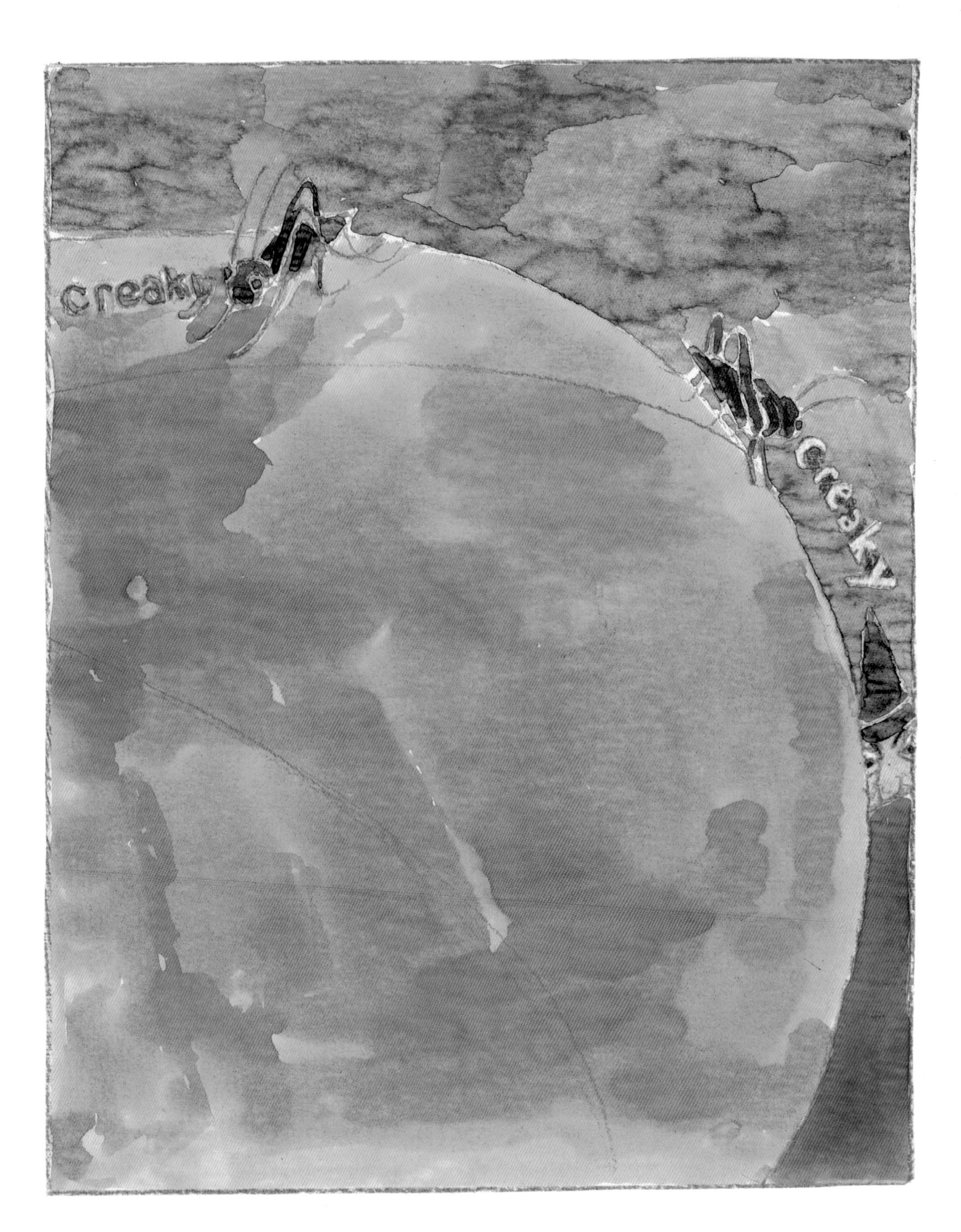
creaky
creaky

I'll take you
and BAKE
you

A witch came *sneaky-sneaky-sneaky.*
"I'll take you and bake you," she said. And she gave it a pat. The pumpkin tried to look very scary. But it just looked big and **FAT**. The witch reached for it. But—

she hid instead. For there came a loud noise.
Girls and boys— searching, seeking, peeking.

OOH
OOOOH

For what? A pumpkin.
They cried *ooh-ooh-ooh* with all their might
because that pumpkin shined so bright.

A girl drew a face on it. Then they carved it carefully.

Triangle eyes that stared.

Raggedy eyebrows that glared.

Jaggedy mouth that grinned.

When they stuck a candle in, the pumpkin shouted *BOO!* with all its might.

BOO!

The owl flew.

The cat fled.

The crickets hurried.

The witch scurried.

The boys and girls ran.

And the jack-o'-lantern laughed out loud,
"How very scary I am!"